williambee

williambee

Stanley's

Diner

Published by
PEACHTREE PUBLISHERS
1700 Chattahoochee Avenue
Atlanta, Georgia 30318-2112
www.peachtree-online.com

First published in Great Britain in 2014 by Jonathan Cape,
an imprint of Random House Children's Publishers UK
First United States version published in 2014 by Peachtree Publishers

The illustrations were rendered digitally.

Printed and bound in March 2015 by Leo Paper Products in China

10 9 8 7 6 5 4 3 2 1 (hardcover)
10 9 8 7 6 5 4 3 2 1 (trade paperback)
First edition

Cataloging-in-Publication Data is available from the Library of Congress.

ISBN 978-1-56145-802-8 (hardcover)
ISBN 978-1-56145-897-4 (trade paperback)

williambee Stanley's Diner

PEACHTREE
ATLANTA

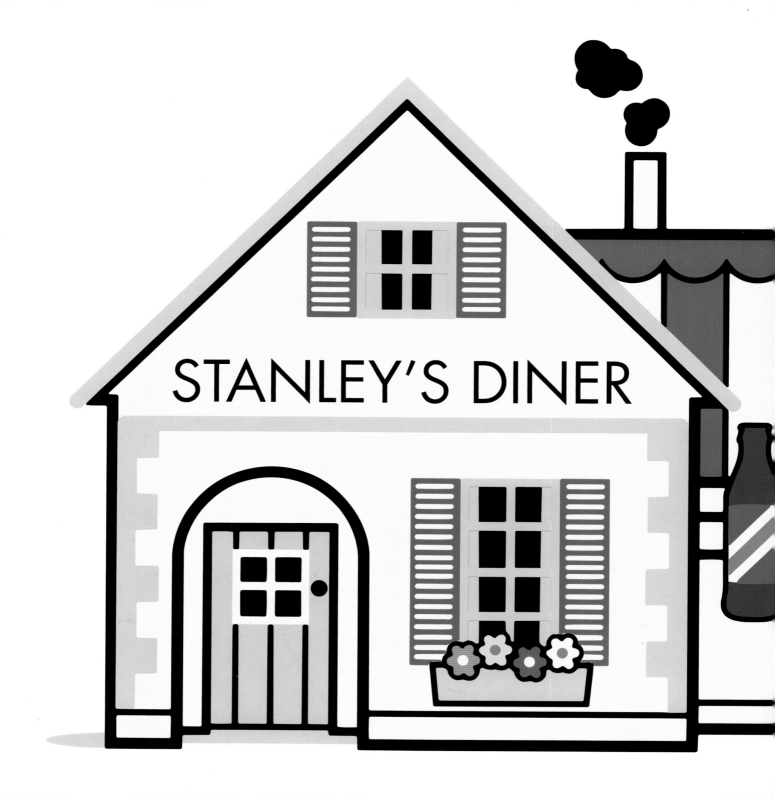

STANLEY'S DINER

It's going to be another busy day
at Stanley's Diner.

What is Stanley doing?

He is in the kitchen cooking eggs, tomatoes, and mushrooms.

Stanley's friend Hattie works in the diner too.
Hattie writes the menu on the blackboard.

Myrtle is here for her breakfast.

She would like eggs and toast, please,
and a cup of coffee.

Stanley has a very big toaster.
Ping! Eight slices all at once!

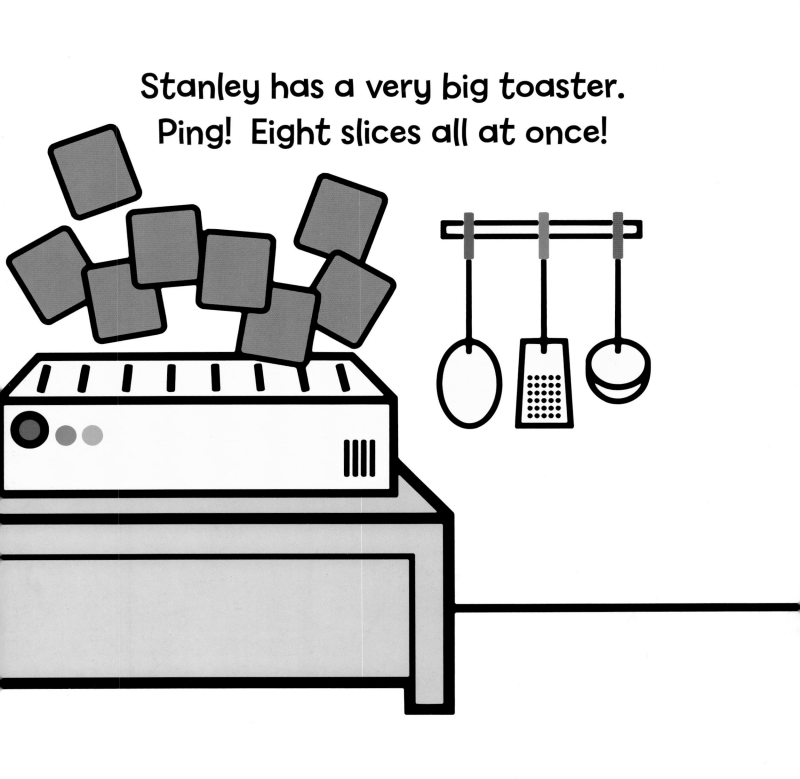

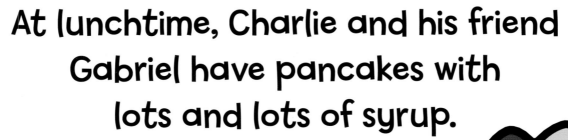

At lunchtime, Charlie and his friend
Gabriel have pancakes with
lots and lots of syrup.

Where has Stanley been in his
pickup truck? He has made
a special trip to the store.

And now he's baking a special cake.
Who could it be for?

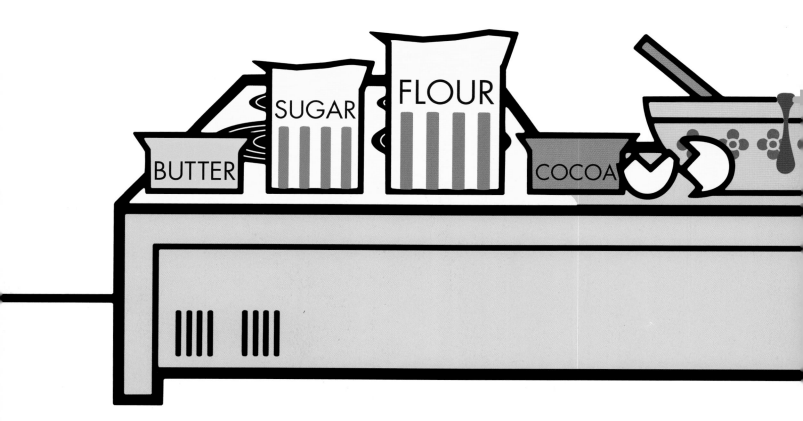

It's for Little Woo. It's his birthday!

Everyone sings,
"Happy Birthday, Little Woo!"
And everyone has a piece of cake. Yum!

Now Stanley cleans up!

Well! What a busy day!

Time for supper!
Time for a bath!

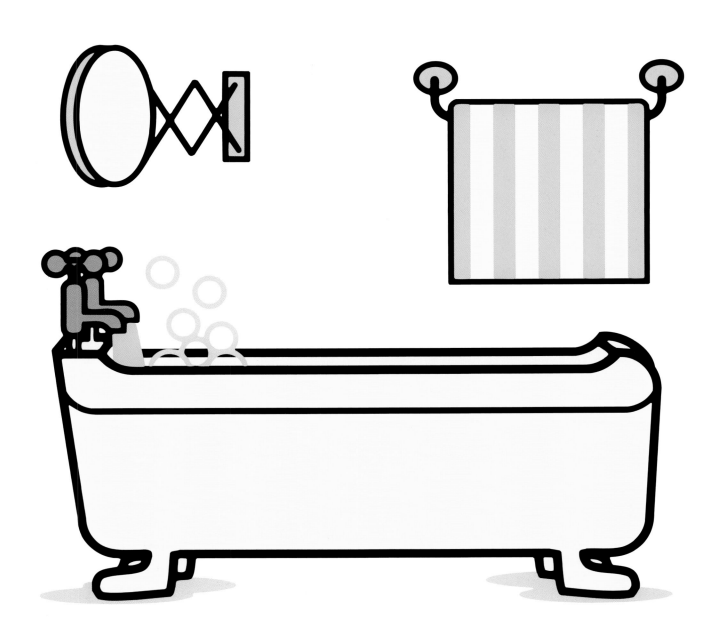

And time for bed!
Goodnight, Stanley.

Stanley

If you liked **Stanley's Diner** then you'll love these other books about Stanley:

Stanley the Builder
Stanley the Farmer
Stanley's Garage

williambee